This Makes Me Scared

DEALING WITH FEELINGS

by Courtney Carbone

illustrated by Hilli Kushnir

Random House

My swim class
begins today.

I am not sure
that I am ready.

The water looks deep.
I cannot see the bottom.

My body is shaking.

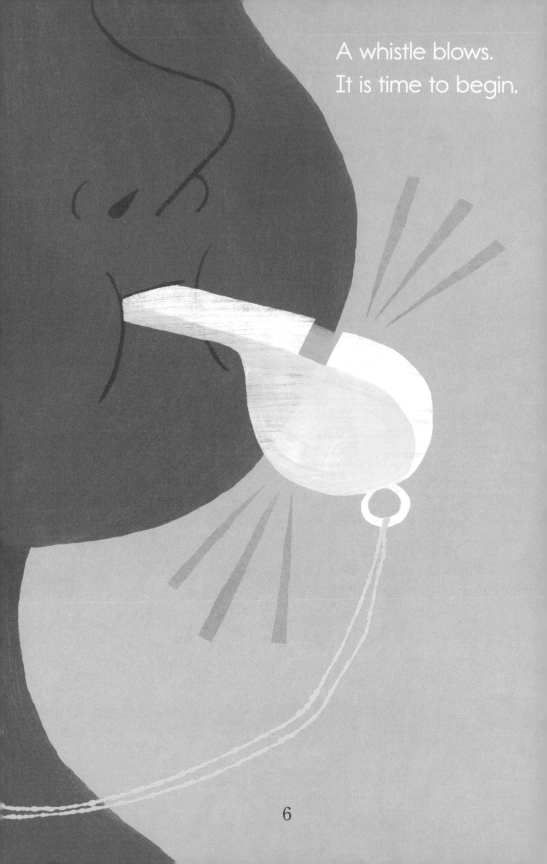

A whistle blows.
It is time to begin.

6

My heart is racing.
Thump, thump, thump!

My teacher shows me how to float.

I try to float.
But I sink instead.

I start to panic.
Water goes up my nose.
I cough and sputter.

I reach for the wall
and hold on tight.

I climb a ladder
out of the pool.

My teacher follows.
She gives me a towel.

She asks me
how I am feeling.

My body is shaking.
My heart is racing.

What am I feeling?
I am feeling *scared.*

My teacher says
it is okay to be scared.

She says we can
face my fear together.

We practice
breathing deeply.

The air goes in and out.
We slowly count to ten.

My mind and body
start to calm down.

I am still scared.
But I am in control.

I am ready to try again.
I get back in the water.
My teacher holds
my hands.

I lie on my back.
I close my eyes.
My teacher slowly
lets go of my hands.

I pretend I am a cloud.
My whole body relaxes.

Soon I am floating!

I did it!
I faced my fear.

I am learning to swim.
Hooray!

For Eric, for diving into this adventure
with me
—C.B.C.

To Liam and Aya, my team of bandits
and partners in crime
—H.K.

Text copyright © 2019 by Courtney Carbone
Cover art and interior illustrations copyright © 2019 by Hilli Kushnir

Visit us on the Web!
StepIntoReading.com
rhcbooks.com

Educators and librarians, for a variety of teaching tools, visit us at
RHTeachersLibrarians.com

Library of Congress Cataloging-in-Publication Data is available upon request.
ISBN 978-0-593-48186-8 (trade) — ISBN 978-0-593-48187-5 (lib. bdg.) —
ISBN 978-0-593-48188-2 (ebook)

Printed in the United States of America
10 9 8 7 6 5 4 3 2 1

This book has been officially leveled by using the F&P Text Level Gradient™ Leveling System.